Dear Parents:

Congratulations! Your child is taking the first steps on an exciting journey. The destination? Independent reading!

STEP INTO READING® will help your child get there. The program offers five steps to reading success. Each step includes fun stories and colorful art or photographs. In addition to original fiction and books with favorite characters, there are Step into Reading Non-Fiction Readers, Phonics Readers and Boxed Sets, Sticker Readers, and Comic Readers—a complete literacy program with something to interest every child.

Learning to Read, Step by Step!

Ready to Read   Preschool   Kindergarten
• big type and easy words • rhyme and rhythm • picture clues
For children who know the alphabet and are eager to begin reading.

Reading with Help   Preschool–Grade 1
• basic vocabulary • short sentences • simple stories
For children who recognize familiar words and sound out new words with help.

Reading on Your Own   Grades 1–3
• engaging characters • easy-to-follow plots • popular topics
For children who are ready to read on their own.

Reading Paragraphs   Grades 2–3
• challenging vocabulary • short paragraphs • exciting stories
For newly independent readers who read simple sentences with confidence.

Ready for Chapters   Grades 2–4
• chapters • longer paragraphs • full-color art
For children who want to take the plunge into chapter books but still like colorful pictures.

STEP INTO READING® is designed to give every child a successful reading experience. The grade levels are only guides; children will progress through the steps at their own speed, developing confidence in their reading.

Remember, a lifetime love of reading starts with a single step!

Copyright © 2014 Disney Enterprises, Inc. All rights reserved. Published in the United States by Random House Children's Books, a division of Random House LLC, 1745 Broadway, New York, NY 10019, and in Canada by Random House of Canada Limited, Toronto, Penguin Random House Companies, in conjunction with Disney Enterprises, Inc.

Step into Reading, Random House, and the Random House colophon are registered trademarks of Random House LLC.

Visit us on the Web!
StepIntoReading.com
randomhouse.com/kids

Educators and librarians, for a variety of teaching tools, visit us at RHTeachersLibrarians.com

ISBN 978-0-7364-3279-5 (trade) — ISBN 978-0-7364-8219-6 (lib. bdg.)
ISBN 978-0-7364-3280-1 (ebook)

Printed in the United States of America
10 9 8 7 6 5 4 3 2

THE CHRISTMAS PARTY

By Andrea Posner-Sanchez

Illustrated by the Disney Storybook Art Team

Random House 🏠 New York

It is almost Christmas!
Elsa invites
the whole kingdom
to celebrate.

5

Elsa uses her magic
to make ice sculptures.
Anna brings out
treats.

Sven helps

decorate the tree.

Kristoff practices
singing carols.

Olaf bakes
Christmas cookies.

Elsa makes sure
he does not get
too close to the oven!

The closets are
stuffed with gifts.

The desserts are ready.

Everything inside
the castle looks great.
Anna wants Elsa
to look outside.

The sisters go
to the window.

The villagers are having fun.

They love
the snow and ice!

"We have worked hard,"
Anna tells Elsa.

"We can have some fun!"

The sisters go outside
to play in the snow.

They have a
snowball fight!

"This is fun!"
says Elsa.
But soon it is time
to get ready
for the party.

Later, Anna knocks
on Elsa's door.
Elsa opens it
and smiles.

Parties are great,
but sisters are the best!